Humpty Dumpty sat on a wall,
Humpty Dumpty had a great fall.
All the King's horses and all the King's men,
Couldn't put Humpty together again.

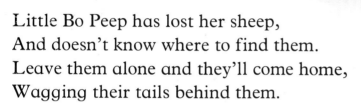

Little Bo Peep has lost her sheep,
And doesn't know where to find them.
Leave them alone and they'll come home,
Wagging their tails behind them.

Little Miss Muffet sat on a tuffet,
Eating her curds and whey.
There came a big spider who sat down beside her,
And frightened Miss Muffet away.

I had a little nut tree, nothing would it bear,
But a silver nutmeg and a golden pear.
The King of Spain's daughter came to visit me,
All for the sake of my little nut tree.

Polly Jumped Over the Moon

1 2 3 4 5 6 7 8 9 10
First American Edition

POLLY
jumped
OVER THE MOON

BY
Helen Solomon
ILLUSTRATED BY
AMELIA ROSATO AND GARY INWOOD

J.B. Lippincott New York

Polly wouldn't speak.
Polly wouldn't sing.
They all tried to teach him,
But he wouldn't say a thing.
"Polly Pretty Polly,"
Said Mommy to the bird,
But Polly looked away,
As if he hadn't even heard.
"Polly, Polly, Polly,
Pretty Polly," Linda said,
But Polly only blinked his eyes
And turned away his head.

Mommy tried to teach him first,
"He'll soon pick up this easy verse,
'Humpty Dumpty sat on the wall,
Humpty Dumpty had a great fall,
All the King's horses and all the King's men,
Couldn't put Humpty together again.'"
But Polly just blinked and that was all.

Then Linda said, "I'll have a go,
Polly will like this one, I know!
'Little Bo Peep has lost her sheep,
And doesn't know where to find them.
Leave them alone and they'll come home,
Wagging their tails behind them!' "
Polly opened his beak!
Was he going to speak?
Mike joined in, "Little Bo Peep."
But Polly simply went to sleep.

So Linda jumped onto a chair,
And, fixing Polly with a glare,
Sang, "Twinkle twinkle little star,
How I wonder what you are.
Up above the world so high,
Like a diamond in the sky."
But Polly wouldn't even try.

Next Mommy tried; "I know a rhyme,
He'll surely say the words this time.
'Little Miss Muffet
Sat on a tuffet,
Eating her curds and whey;
There came a big spider,
Who sat down beside her,
And frightened Miss Muffet away.'"
But not a word would Polly say.

Mike said, "I think it's my turn.
I know a rhyme that he could learn.
'I had a little nut tree,
Nothing would it bear,
But a silver nutmeg and a golden pear.
The King of Spain's daughter came to visit me,
All for the sake of my little nut tree.'
Oh Polly," Mike cried sadly,
"Why won't you look at me?"

"Don't shout at him!" said Daddy, "Now,
That's not the way to teach him how.
I know some good rhymes, too.
'Cock-a-doodle-doo,
My dame has lost her shoe.
My master's lost his fiddling stick,
And doesn't know what to do.' "
"It's no good, Dad," said Linda.
"He's turned his back on you."

On lots of days they said their rhymes,
And sometimes they would sing.
But Polly simply tucked his head
Underneath his wing.
Sometimes Polly nodded.
Sometimes Polly turned his head,
As if he had not heard.
He winked at them.
He blinked at them.
But never said a word.

Then Mommy began to sing one day,
"Hey diddle diddle,
The cat and the fiddle . . . "
"Hey!" squawked Polly, "Hey!"
"What did he say? Did he say 'Hey'?"
Mike and Linda cried.
Polly stared at them.
Polly glared at them.
Then turned away and sighed.
Mom told them both to go away.
"Leave it to me," she said.
"I'll teach him to speak,
He'll soon open his beak.
He'll be talking by Christmas Day."

On Christmas Day
Polly opened his beak . . .
Would he speak?
"Polly," Mommy coaxed him,
And gently stroked his head.
He blinked.
He winked.
And this is what he said . . .

"Twinkle twinkle, black sheep,
Sitting on a wall,
With Little Bo Peep-peep,
He had a great fall.
I had a little nut tree,
Eating curds and whey,
A spider came to marry me
And frightened Miss Mufferty away.
Humperty – Dumperty –
Mufferty – Dufferty –

Hanging out the clothes
With rings on all her fingers
And bells on all her toes.
With a pocket full of rye
Like a diamond in the sky,
Little Bo Peep-peep
Peep-er-peep----
Lost her shoe!
Cock-a-doodle-doo!"

"Don't you worry," Mommy said.
"The rhymes are muddled in his head.
He'll get them right quite soon."
"Yes!" squawked Polly loudly,
"And Polly jumped over the moon!"

Baa, baa, black sheep, have you any wool?
Yes sir, yes sir, three bags full.
One for my master and one for my dame,
And one for the little boy who lives down the lane.

Ride a cockhorse to Banbury Cross,
To see a fine lady ride on a white horse.
With rings on her fingers and bells on her toes,
She shall have music wherever she goes.

Hey diddle diddle, the cat and the fiddle,
The cow jumped over the moon.
The little dog laughed to see such fun,
And the dish ran away with the spoon.

Sing a song of sixpence, a pocket full of rye;
Four and twenty blackbirds baked in a pie.
When the pie was opened the birds began to sing.
Wasn't that a dainty dish to set before the king?